EXTREME HABITATS

POLAR REGIONS

EMILY KINGTON

hungrytomato.com

Victoria House, Staplefield Lane,
Staplefield, West Sussex, UK

First published by
Hungry Tomato Ltd in 2021,
F1, Old Bakery Studios,
Blewetts Wharf, Malpas Road,
Truro, Cornwall, TR1 1QH, UK

ISBN 978 1 914087 06 6

Manufactured in the USA

A CIP catalogue record for this book is available from the British Library.

Picture credits
(t = top, b = bottom, m = middle, l = left, r = right, bg = background)

Alamy Pictorial Press/Alamy 19tl. Arctic Photo 6l, 6br, 7ml, 10bl, 11mr, 12b, 13t, 21ml, 21tr, 25br, 26tl, 27t, 27tr, 27mr. blickwinkel/Alamy 15t. Corbis Galen Rowell/Corbis 17tl. Cosmographics 26bl. Edwin Mickleburgh/Ardea 25mr. Kim Westerskov/Getty 10tl. NASA 19mr, 25tl, 29bl, 29bm. Rick Price/Corbis 25mr. Rozet/Jupiter Images 20tr; Shutterstock: 5mr; 9t; 9mr; 11m; 13mr; 14l; 15mr; 16b; 20mr; 20br; 21mr; 21br; 23mr; Alena NV 5bm; Andre Nantel 14m; Angelica Klingberg 23br; Danita Delimont (front cover); David Dennis 15b; Designua 16tl; EvgenyPlotnikov 2bg; Gail Johnson 23tr; gillmar 13br; Henning Janos 11bm; Jeff R. Clow 29m; Joy Brown 29mb; Kris Grabiec 4bg; Melissa King 7br; Myeongho Seo 8bg; NaturesMomentsuk 18bg; Nik Niklz 23b; Nishi's Images 28tl; Petr Simon 9br; PICARD Gweg 22tl; rangsan paidaen (fact file); richardjohnson 22br; Risto Raunio 16bg; Risto Raunio 1bg; Robert St-Coeur 17br; Roman Krochuk 17t; Rudmer Zwerver 7tm; sinoptic (notebook and tips illustrations); Tarpan 24tl; Tory Kallman 25tr; vladsilver 12tl; Yegor Larin 10bg. tbkmedia.de/Alamy 25mr. Zachary Staniszewski 19b.

Every effort has been made to trace the copyright holders, and we apologise in advance for any unintentional omissions.
We would be pleased to insert the appropriate acknowledgments in any subsequent edition of this publication.

CONTENTS

THE ENDS OF THE EARTH

If you're looking for an extreme habitat, head for the ends of the Earth – the poles. Bright, white snow and ice stretch far into the distance in some of the harshest places on Earth.

This map shows the Arctic Circle. Everything inside of this circle is considered to be in the Arctic.

There are two polar regions. They are the coldest, driest and windiest places on Earth. Temperatures can drop to a brain-numbing -76°F (-60°C).

The **Arctic** is the name given to the area around the **North Pole**. There is no land underneath most of the Arctic – it is just a giant, floating sheet of ice on top of the **Arctic Ocean**.

Map showing the Antarctic region.

The **Antarctic** is the frozen land near the **South Pole**. Even in summer, most of the land is covered with thick ice. Very few plants and animals can survive the incredible cold, but some have adapted to life there.

POLAR SURVIVAL TIPS

The air at the poles is very dry. You will need to drink several pints of water a day to avoid **dehydration**.

POLAR NOTEBOOK

- Antarctica is the fifth largest **continent**. Only Europe and Australia are smaller. Antarctica is one and a half times the size of the USA.
- When temperatures drop to -94°F (-70°C), your breath freezes. It falls to the ground with a noise some people call "the whispering of the stars".

WITH A COMPASS, A TRAVELER CAN ALWAYS FIND NORTH.

- Compasses work using a needle that points towards the **magnetic North Pole**.
- The magnetic North Pole is about 1,000 miles (1,600 kilometers) south of the geographic North Pole. The magnetic pole is not fixed in one place, but moves slowly all the time.

POLAR EXPLORER

A trip to either pole is like visiting another planet. You can watch giant icebergs float by, climb jagged mountains, sail past huge cliffs of ice, or just gaze at the empty, icy landscape.

This Sami woman from the Arctic is wearing traditional reindeer skin clothes.

It's vital to keep warm and dry. Wear lots of layers to trap warm air, and cover these with a thick jacket to protect yourself from the wind.

Choose boots with rough soles and spikes to grip the icy ground.

Forgot to pack your tent? Don't worry – an igloo provides shelter from freezing winds.

Igloos are traditional shelters made from blocks of ice stacked tightly together to form a dome.

Although igloos are made from snow and ice, they are warm inside.

POLAR SURVIVAL TIPS

If you see a skua - duck! These vicious birds will attack you with their feet. It feels like being hit by a frozen chicken!

Scientists drill into the ice in Antarctica to take samples of the ice many feet down. They study changes in the ice over time.

POLAR NOTEBOOK

- The cold is dangerous. If your body temperature drops below 89.6°F (32°C) you could die.

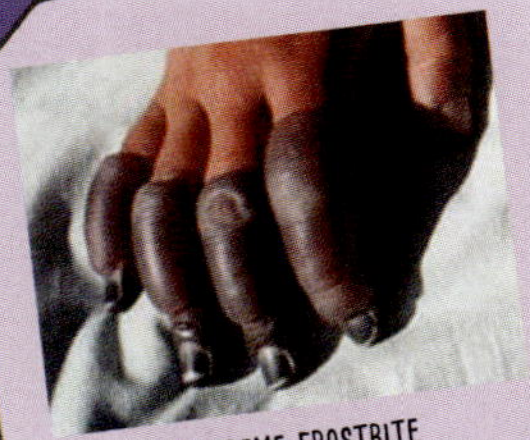

EXTREME FROSTBITE

- When your body freezes, the skin becomes black and swollen. This is frostbite. In very extreme cases, doctors are unable to save body parts affected by frostbite.

Polar explorers need a lot of equipment. Before you go you must make sure you have the essentials:

- Warm clothing and boots
- Tent and sleeping bags
- Food supplies (dried foods are lighter)
- Small cooking stove and fuel
- Rope, ice axe, snow shovel
- Skis, snow shoes
- Maps, compass and satellite phone

Use a snowmobile to travel around the Arctic.

THE COLDEST PLACE ON EARTH

Look inside your freezer and think what it would be like to live in an icy, cold place. The Antarctic is the coldest place on Earth. If you threw boiling water in the air here, it would freeze instantly.

The Antarctic is a lot colder than the Arctic. This is because the Antarctic is land that has hundreds of feet of ice on top of it. The ice at the Arctic is much thinner. Currents of warm water flow into the Arctic Ocean and keep the temperatures there slightly higher.

Several species of penguin live in the Antarctic, but it is only Emperor penguins that have their chicks during the bitter Antarctic winter.

WHY IS IT SO COLD?

The poles are cold because they never face the Sun directly. The Sun's rays are weaker and more spread out at the poles than they are at the Equator.

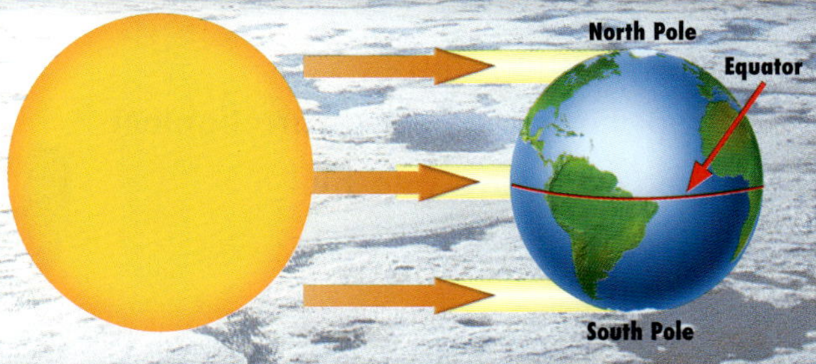

Most mountains on Antarctica are buried under the ice. Only a few peaks stick out, known as nanataks.

POLAR NOTEBOOK

- The coldest temperature ever recorded was in 1983 in Antarctica – a bone-chilling -128.6 °F (-89.2 °C).
- In autumn, the Antarctic sea ice grows at a rate of 2.5 miles (4 kilometers) a day.

IN AUTUMN THIS SEA WILL FREEZE OVER.

- When the sea freezes, Antarctica doubles in size. It takes just two and a half weeks for this to happen.

Antarctica's snow reflects the sunlight, making it very cold. Another reason for the cold is its **elevation**.

The average height above **sea level** is 8,200 feet (2,500 meters) – three times higher than any other continent in the world.

POLAR SURVIVAL TIPS

Wear sunglasses or dark goggles. **Snowblindness**, caused by looking at bright white snow for too long, can seriously damage your eyes.

The Arctic tern travels between the Arctic and Antarctic, making a round trip of 22,000 miles (35,000 kilometers) every year.

THE FROZEN KINGDOM

The US ship Healy is used for polar research, and for cutting a path through the ice for other ships.

The edge of the Arctic Circle is almost completely ringed by land, including parts of Canada, Alaska, Russia and Greenland. The center of the Arctic is sea, with a permanent layer of ice over the coldest parts.

Ships called 'ice breakers' smash their way through the sea ice. The shape of the ship pushes it up onto the ice. Then its weight forces the ice to split and creates a path.

In summer, the Arctic ice shrinks. Around the edges, it breaks up into large sheets of ice. These sheets are separated by channels of water known as leads.

Arctic scientists uncover their sledge after a blizzard.

In polar regions, glare from dazzling snow can play tricks on your mind. You lose your sense of up, down, far and near. It can cause plane accidents, and explorers to have falls. Even birds fly into the ground!

In 1997, three skydivers died after failing to open their parachutes. They didn't realize they were so close to the ground.

These skydivers wear skis to help them land on the Arctic snow.

POLAR NOTEBOOK

- On average, the Arctic ice is 10 to 16 feet (3-5 meters) thick.
- The Arctic ice covers 6 million square miles (15.6 million square kilometers) of sea in winter, but shrinks to 2.5 million square miles (6.5 million square kilometers) in summer.
- Polar explorers often don't wash at all, it's too chilly! Melting ice to make water also wastes fuel. Luckily the cold, dry air means they don't smell too bad.

RUSSIAN HOUSES IN THE ARCTIC.

- Arctic houses are built on wooden stilts, some up to 50 feet (15 meters) tall. Otherwise, the warm houses would melt the frozen ground below and sink into the Earth!

POLAR SURVIVAL TIPS

Take care! Ice may look smooth but it is actually rough, and can cut you if you fall. Sharp ice crystals can be seen under a microscope.

THE WILDEST WINDS

Emperor penguin chicks shelter together in big huddles, surviving howling gales and temperatures of -76°F (-60°C).

The hurricane-force winds at the poles make life almost unbearable. Winds start and stop suddenly, which could cause you to fall flat on your face.

The wind drives snow into every crack of your clothing, even inside your watch. The driving snow causes **white-outs**, where all you can see in any direction is white. It is said by some explorers to be like walking inside a ping-pong ball!

Arctic explorers shelter in tents. During this storm, the winds reached 68 miles (110 kilometers) per hour.

Arctic weather stations record temperature and wind speed. Equipment can be hard to find in the snow. Here, flags mark the spot.

Antarctica has the strongest winds in the world. In hilly areas, **katabatic** winds blow at speeds up to 200 miles (320 kilometers) per hour. They come in short, sudden blasts that can rip a tent apart.

The stronger the wind, the more quickly your body loses heat. This is known as the **windchill factor**. Every extra two kilometers per hour in wind speed means your body drops 1.8 °F (1 °C) in temperature.

POLAR NOTEBOOK

- Some polar explorers use **huskies** to pull their sleds.
- During storms, a husky will curl up into a tight ball with its back to the wind.

A HUSKY'S THICK FUR PROTECTS IT DURING A BLIZZARD.

- Even in poor conditions, a team of huskies can usually pull a sled at around 6 to 7 miles (9.7-11 kilometers) per hour.

POLAR SURVIVAL TIPS

Don't use ponies to pull your sled.
A pony sweats through its body. The sweat freezes into a blanket of ice, which could kill it.
Huskies only sweat through their tongues.

Only a small part of an iceberg can be seen above the water.

DEADLY SEAS

If you're sailing in polar waters, keep an eye on the weather. Storms can appear from nowhere. Towering waves can toss a ship from side to side. You will also need to watch out for icebergs.

All **icebergs** are dangerous to ships. They can be hard to spot, particularly in foggy conditions. The International Ice Patrol protects shipping in the Arctic. They track dangerous icebergs and warn ships of their position.

A beluga whale swimming in the Arctic Ocean.

In summer, the Arctic Ocean is one of the most humid places on Earth. The air feels even wetter than in the Amazon rainforest. Dense fogs rise from the sea and wrap the ice in a thick white blanket.

Ships in the Antarctic also face foggy conditions.

Early Arctic Ocean explorers only had small boats, which placed them in great danger from whales. Today, the opposite is true. Up to a third of dead whales show signs of having been struck by ships.

POLAR NOTEBOOK

- Icebergs drift at a speed of around 1,640 feet (500 meters) an hour.
- Most icebergs melt fairly quickly. But in 1926, one Arctic iceberg got within 155 miles (250 kilometers) of the tropical island of Bermuda.

BERMUDA IS OVER 2,500 MILES (4,000 KILOMETERS) AWAY FROM THE ARCTIC.

- Ice can be noisy! In spring, the Arctic is filled with loud creaks and cracks as the ice shifts around.

POLAR SURVIVAL TIPS

Keep away from the edge of an ice shelf. These huge white cliffs can be dangerous. Huge lumps of ice can suddenly break off and fall on to your boat.

THE LONGEST DAY

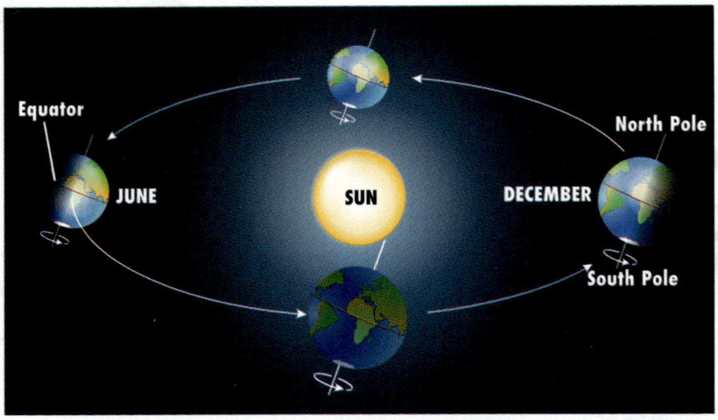

This diagram shows how the Earth's tilt affects the light at the poles. In June, the North Pole is tilted towards the Sun, so light falls on the Arctic day and night. The South Pole is tilted away and remains in darkness. The opposite is true for December.

Can you imagine living in daylight for months on end? There is only one day and one night each year at the North and South Poles. Each lasts six months.

In the polar summer, the Sun never sets. It is called the 'midnight Sun'. During winter, the Sun never rises. This is known as the 'polar night'. Without daylight, the world is dark and very, very cold.

When it is always light, how would you divide up your days? The reindeer that live in the Arctic ditch their daily routines. They simply take naps whenever they feel like them.

During the polar summer the Sun comes close to the horizon, but never actually sets.

POLAR SURVIVAL TIPS

Fire is an important source of warmth and light in polar regions. But watch out! Fires burn fiercely in the dry polar air.

In the Arctic, the aurora are also called the Northern Lights.

During the winter, **aurora** light up the polar skies. These dancing curtains of light stretch hundreds of miles across the sky. They are caused by particles from the Sun hitting Earth's atmosphere.

POLAR NOTEBOOK

- The polar skies sometimes cause **mirages**. Objects such as islands, cliffs and ships appear to be floating above the ground.
- You can sometimes see huge pillars of light stretching into the sky. They are caused by light from the Sun or Moon reflecting off ice crystals.

PILLARS OF LIGHT

- Many astronomers work at the poles. There is very little pollution in the sky, so they can see the stars clearly.

THE LONELIEST PLACE IN THE WORLD

The Amundsen-Scott Research Station at the South Pole.

The polar landscape can be beautiful, peaceful, wild and terrifying. It can also be very, very boring. Imagine being cooped up in a few small buildings for months with nowhere to go!

There are many **research stations** in the Antarctic. They are equipped with living, sleeping and eating quarters as well as science laboratories and libraries. Some stations are built underground – though every few years they risk getting crushed by the weight of moving ice.

More researchers live in the Antarctic in the summer. For instance, there are sometimes up to 200 people at the Amundsen-Scott station during the summer, but most leave in the winter before the weather makes travel impossible.

Some Antarctic scientists study the ice or the plants, while others look at the weather conditions and pollution.

POLAR SURVIVAL TIPS

Going out for a walk? Hang on tight to the survival rope linked to the station. Without the rope it's easy to get lost.

In 1911, Roald Amundsen (right) and Robert Falcon Scott raced each other to become the first explorers to reach the South Pole. The Amundsen-Scott Research Station is named after the two men.

The information they discover is helping scientists around the world to understand how the planet is changing because of **global warming**.

This plane is equipped with skis to land on the icy ground of the South Pole. It makes regular supply trips to the scientists during the summer season.

POLAR NOTEBOOK

- Antarctica is very remote. The nearest big bit of land is the southern tip of South America, over 600 miles (960 kilometers) away.
- The first explorers arrived in Antarctica about 200 years ago.

NASA ASTRONAUT

- Some NASA astronauts do part of their training in Antarctica. The long winters prepare them for dark, lonely journeys in space.

FACT FILE:

PLANT SURVIVORS

Only the world's toughest plants can survive the fierce winds, freezing cold, and dark winter months of the polar lands.

Plants such as bearberries are an important source of food for many Arctic animals.

- During winter, both the Arctic and the Antarctic are wild and barren, with almost no life.
- Moss, grass, **pearlwort, algae** and **lichen** are the only plants to grow in the Antarctic.
- The Antarctic is so cold that plants grow very slowly. Mosses grow as much in a year as your fingernails do in a week!
- The **tundra** (the land that lies nearest to the Arctic) bursts into life during the short summer.
- Arctic plants are small, grow close together and remain close to the ground. This protects them from the strong winds and the cold.
- Some plants have dark flowers or leaves that absorb the heat of the Sun.

Lichens growing on rock.

Dark leaves absorb sunlight better than pale leaves.

FACT FILE

- Some Arctic plants, such as the dwarf willow, are covered in tiny hairs that keep them warm, like a woolly jumper.
- Arctic flowers grow quickly. They must bloom and produce seeds before the winter returns.

The Arctic tundra in summer.

This chart shows the summer months in the Arctic and Antarctic.

ARCTIC	ANTARCTIC
JANUARY	**JANUARY**
FEBRUARY	**FEBRUARY**
MARCH	MARCH
APRIL	APRIL
MAY	MAY
JUNE	**JUNE**
JULY	**JULY**
AUGUST	**AUGUST**
SEPTEMBER	SEPTEMBER
OCTOBER	OCTOBER
NOVEMBER	NOVEMBER
DECEMBER	DECEMBER

Key: Winter = Summer =

ARCTIC PLANTS

Arctic willow

- Grows along the ground to avoid the wind.
- Can grow to over 16 feet (5 meters) long.
- Its branches are never more than 4 inches (10 centimeters) above the ground.

Arctic poppies

- Cup-shaped flowers that direct the Sun's rays towards the center of the flower.
- Their shape allows these plants to stay warmer than the air around them.

Cotton grass

- Uses the Arctic winds to blow its seeds far and wide.
- Local people, the Inuits, use the silky 'cotton' at the top of the plant to stuff pillows and mattresses.

Arctic willow

Arctic poppies

Cotton grass

ARCTIC ANIMAL SURVIVORS

AN ARCTIC FOX IN WINTER.

There are no animals that live in the very far north of the Arctic. But the land and sea within the Arctic Circle are full of life. You will find reindeer, foxes and lemmings on the land, and fish, seals and whales in the sea.

- Large bodies hold in heat better than small ones. So many polar animals are big, such as musk oxen and reindeer.
- Some Arctic animals have a very thick layer of fat under the skin to keep them warm. This is called **blubber**.
- During the winter months, when it is hard to find food, animals can live off the blubber they have stored.
- Arctic animals such as polar bears and foxes have thick fur coats.
- Birds, such as snow geese, visit the Arctic tundra during the summer to feed on the insects that breed there.
- Every year, more than a million reindeer move north and arrive in the Arctic Circle in the summer. There they can feed day and night, thanks to the 24 hour sunshine of the midnight Sun.

Walruses have so much blubber they get too hot when they come on land!

FACT FILE

Arctic Survivors

Walrus

- Uses its big whiskers to feel for shellfish on the seabed.
- Its tough head can knock a hole in ice that is up to 8 inches (20 cm) thick.

Walrus

Reindeer

- Both males and females have antlers. They use them to scrape snow away from the ground to find food.
- Broad feet stop reindeer from sinking into the snow.

Reindeer

Arctic fox

- Thick, hairy foot pads grip the ice.
- During the autumn, its coat turns from brown to white so it can hide in the snow.

Lemmings

- Dig a network of tunnels in the snow.
- Live on plants they find beneath the snow.

Lemming

How do Polar bears survive in the Arctic?

FACT FILE

Most Krill grow to between 0.4 to 0.8 inches (1-2 centimeters) long. They feed on algae.

BELOW THE ANTARCTIC ICE

Most of Antarctica is covered with ice. It is just too cold and dry for animals to live here, but there is life in the ocean and on the ice close to the sea.

- Several species of bird have adapted to life in Antarctica. Colonies of penguins live along the rocky coastlines. Seabirds such as petrels and skuas hunt for fish here.
- Under the ice, the waters are full of life. Fish, whales, crabs and other creatures swim in the dark, cold depths.
- Some polar animals living in the sea grow to giant size. This is because the more oxygen they get, the bigger they can grow. Cold water has more oxygen in it than warm water and so the cold polar oceans have a lot of oxygen.
- In the summer, the Antarctic seas are filled with swarms of shrimp-like creatures called krill.
- Orcas are the largest predators in the Antarctic waters. They are clever hunters. An orca will tip up small icebergs to knock resting seals into the water.
- Lake Vostok lies in the heart of the Antarctic, buried under 2.5 miles (4 kilometers) of ice. The water in the lake is cold and very dark. It is like Europa, one of Jupiter's moons. Perhaps if we found life in Lake Vostok, we might find alien life on Europa.

FACT FILE

Orcas (killer whales) prefer cooler waters, and are found in both the Arctic and Antarctic.

MONSTERS OF THE DEEP

Giant woodlice

- Grow up to 8 inches (20 centimeters) long.
- They are scavengers and eat the remains of any dead animal they come across.

Giant woodlouse

Sea spiders

- Grow to the size of a dinner plate.
- Weigh up to 1,000 times as much as sea spiders in warmer waters.
- Bright orange in color with 10-12 legs.
- Live in deep Antarctic waters and feed on sea anemones.

Sea spider

Ice fish

- Make their own **antifreeze** to allow their blood to stay liquid when most other animal bodies would freeze solid.
- Large eyes help them hunt in the dark waters.

Ice fish

Weddell seals

- Spend long periods under the ice.
- They gnaw at the ice with their teeth to keep air holes open to breathe.
- Can stay below surface for up to 70 minutes and can dive to depths of 1,900 feet (580 meters).

Weddell seal

TRADITIONAL SAMI CLOTHING IS RED AND BLUE, AND DECORATED WITH YELLOW OR WHITE.

ARCTIC PEOPLE

Even today, nobody lives in the Antarctic for more than a few years at a time. However, people have made their homes in the Arctic for 15,000 years.

Where Arctic people live

PEOPLE	COUNTRY
EVENKS	RUSSIA
INUIT	GREENLAND, CANADA, ALASKA AND RUSSIA
NENETS	RUSSIA
SAMI	FINLAND, NORWAY, SWEDEN AND RUSSIA

- Many groups of people live in the Arctic, including the Inuit and Nenets. Each group has its own language and customs.
- The Inuit hunt many animals, including walruses, polar bears, reindeer, seals and geese. The animals are used for food, shelter, clothing and weapons.
- The Inuit used to make seal-skin boots and line them with moss and dry grass for extra **insulation**.
- The Nenets and Sami traditionally lived nomadic lives. They followed their giant herds of reindeer across the Arctic, eating their meat, milk and cheese and using their skins

for clothes and other goods. Tents made from reindeer skins were light and easy to carry around.

- Today most Arctic people get around on snowmobiles and live in modern houses with central heating.

A Sami woman with a herd of reindeer.

SURVIVAL TECHNIQUES

Igloos

- Igloos are temporary shelters that can be quickly built from the ice.
- They are surprisingly warm inside.
- The inner walls are covered in snow, which melts then freezes into a smooth covering of ice.

Snow glare

- Goggles protect your eyes from the glare of the snow. The Inuits used to make them from reindeer skin.

Balanced diet

- Early explorers to the Arctic often suffered from scurvy, an illness that comes from not getting enough Vitamin C.
- The Inuit knew to eat raw meat, which contains Vitamin C.

Igloo

Reindeer skin goggles

Raw seal meat can prevent scurvy

FACT FILE

THE MELTING OF THE POLAR ICE MAKES IT DIFFICULT FOR REINDEER TO TRAVEL NORTH TO THEIR TRADITIONAL FEEDING PLACES IN THE ARCTIC.

POLES IN DANGER

In the last few decades, the world has become warmer. Global warming has caused the polar ice to shrink, causing hardship for polar animals, particularly those in the Arctic.

- Although the poles are at the far ends of the world, we are having a big effect on them. As the world warms up, the ice at the poles is beginning to melt.
- Sea ice is melting earlier in the year. Without large sheets of ice to travel over, polar bears have trouble reaching the seals they eat as their main source of food.
- If the polar ice melted completely, the sea would rise by 160 feet (50 meters). This would flood the coasts. Many large cities would be affected, including London, New York, Mumbai and Tokyo.
- The poles are a good place to study our planet because they are so clean and unspoilt. Any pollution can be measured easily.
- No one owns Antarctica, but 48 countries around the world have agreed to protect the continent.
- The 1961 Antarctic Treaty allows all scientists to work in Antarctica, but only if they do not conduct tests that would harm the environment.
- Strict laws for scientists and tourists in polar areas help to protect the unique habitat.

FACT FILE

Polar Problems

Drilling

- Drilling for oil brings roads, houses and pipelines into the Arctic.
- These can block the traditional routes which reindeer use to move across the Arctic.
- The change in reindeer behavior affects the animals that hunt them, such as wolves.
- A damaged oil pipe can spill millions of gallons of oil, killing hundreds of birds, fish and mammals.

Over-fishing

- Large numbers of fish and squid are taken from the polar seas.
- Over-fishing reduces the food for animals such as dolphins, seals and penguins.

Oil pipes in Alaska

Oil spills kill wildlife

Over-fishing

These pictures show the Arctic ice cover in 1979 and 2005. They show how ice has melted away during that time. It continues to melt more and more each year.

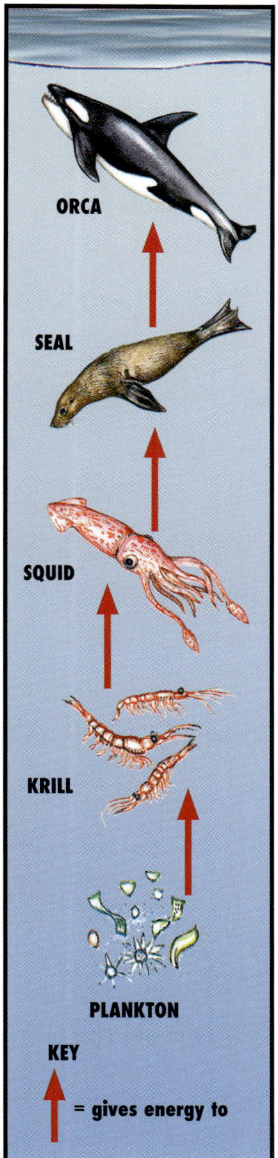

This simple food chain shows how larger creatures depend on smaller creatures for food. If pollution affects one link in the chain, it can damage many other animals.

GLOSSARY

algae – simple plants that live in water, many of which can only be seen with a microscope.

Antarctic – the area surrounding the South Pole. Antarctica is a continent, but it is not owned by any country. Instead it is protected by international laws.

antifreeze – something that stops liquid, such as blood, from freezing.

Arctic – the area within the Arctic Circle. Most of the Arctic is sea and ice, but there is some land, including parts of Russia, Canada, Greenland and Alaska.

Arctic Ocean – the ocean surrounding the Arctic. Much of the sea is covered in ice. The Arctic Ocean is about one and a half times the size of the USA.

astronomers – people who study outer space.

aurora – lights in the polar sky caused by particles from the Sun reacting to Earth's atmosphere.

blubber – a thick layer of fat beneath the skin that protects an animal from the cold. For some Arctic animals, blubber is half of their body weight.

continent – a huge area of land, such as Europe, North America or Antarctica.

dehydration – to become ill because your body does not have enough water.

elevation – the height of something above sea level.

Equator – an imaginary line around the Earth, dividing the world into a northern half and southern half.

frostbite – the damage to skin caused by intense cold.

global warming – the increase in Earth's temperature, caused by pollution in the atmosphere.

humid – a large amount of water vapor in the air.

huskies – a breed of dog that is adapted to survive in polar conditions.

iceberg – ice that is not attached to land.

ice shelf – a sheet of ice that forms over the water and is attached to the land.

insulation – a material that is used to protect something from the cold.

katabatic – a strong wind that blows down a mountain.

leads – channels of seawater that can

be seen in the gap between sheets of ice.

lichen – a simple plant that grows on rocks and takes its nutrients from the air.

magnetic North Pole – the place where compass needles point. It is caused by the shape of Earth's magnetic fields. The magnetic North Pole is not in the same place as the true North Pole.

mirages – tricks of the light that cause you to see things that are not there.

nanataks – mountains that are mostly under ice, so only the very tops can be seen poking through the snow.

North Pole – the point on Earth that is farthest north.

pearlwort – a plant that lives in the Antarctic. It looks like moss.

research station – buildings where scientists live and work.

sea level – the sea's surface. It is used as a starting point for measuring the height of mountains.

snowblindness – damage to the eyes caused by the glare of the Sun on bright white snow.

snowmobiles – motor vehicles used for traveling over the snow and ice.

South Pole – the point on Earth that is farthest south.

stilts – long, strong poles that support something above the ground.

tundra – the vast flat land in the Arctic, where it is too cold for any trees to grow.

unique – unlike anything else.

white-outs – weather conditions such as a heavy snow blizzard that cause you to only see white.

windchill factor – the temperature that you feel, which is a combination of air temperature and wind speed.

INDEX